SUPER TURBO

GETS CAUGHT

By Lee Kirby
Illustrated by George O'Connor

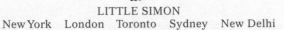

LITTLE SIMON

New York   London   Toronto   Sydney   New Delhi

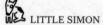 LITTLE SIMON

An imprint of Simon & Schuster Children's Publishing Division • 1230 Avenue of the Americas, New York, New York 10020 • First Little Simon hardcover edition November 2018. Copyright © 2018 by Simon & Schuster, Inc. All rights reserved, including the right of reproduction in whole or in part in any form. LITTLE SIMON is a registered trademark of Simon & Schuster, Inc., and associated colophon is a trademark of Simon & Schuster, Inc. For information about special discounts for bulk purchases, please contact Simon & Schuster Special Sales at 1-866-506-1949 or business@simonandschuster.com. The Simon & Schuster Speakers Bureau can bring authors to your live event. For more information or to book an event contact the Simon & Schuster Speakers Bureau at 1-866-248-3049 or visit our website at www.simonspeakers.com. Designed by Jay Colvin. The text of this book was set in Little Simon Gazette.

Manufactured in the United States of America 1018 FFG 10 9 8 7 6 5 4 3 2 1

Cataloging-in-Publication Data for this title is available from the Library of Congress.

ISBN 978-1-5344-2986-4 (hc)

ISBN 978-1-5344-2985-7 (pbk)

ISBN 978-1-5344-2987-1 (eBook)

CONTENTS

1

THE MYSTERIOUS, SHADOWY FIGURE

It was late at night. The school lights were out. All the kids and teachers had gone home hours ago so the hallways were empty. Empty except for one mysterious, shadowy figure. But no matter. Moving on—

Hey, wait a second. A mysterious, shadowy figure? Something big and

secret is going on here.
But it's not the *original*
big secret. That secret is
about this little guy right
here.

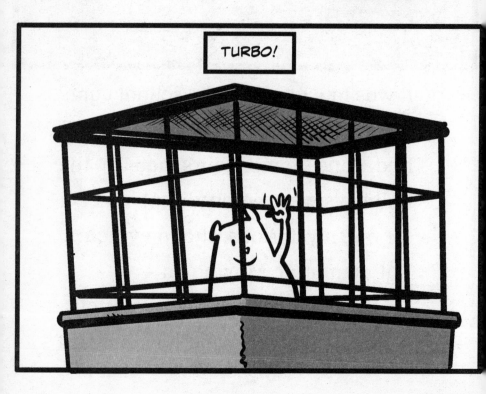

TURBO!

The secret is that he's not just a regular hamster named Turbo. Because he's actually . . .

SUPER TURBO! OFFICIAL CLASS PET OF CLASSROOM C, BUT ALSO A SUPERPET! WITH SUPERPOWERS! AND A NIFTY CAPE AND GOGGLES!

But at the moment, Turbo was nowhere in sight. So back to that Mysterious Shadowy Figure.

The Mysterious, Shadowy Figure made his way down the darkened hallway. The figure had some small cages tucked under his arm.

Every few feet, he would leave one of the cages on the floor.

2

THE NEWEST SUPERPET

Normally that kind of shady, shadowy behavior is exactly the sort of thing Super Turbo would have jumped on. Unfortunately, Super Turbo was busy at the time. To be specific, he and the rest of Sunnyview Elementary's Superpet Superhero League were holding a top-secret meeting in their usual meeting space: the cozy reading nook of Classroom C.

Boy, there sure were lots of secretive things happening!

In case you need a refresher on the Superpet Superhero League, here are the members.

LEO, AKA THE GREAT GECKO. OFFICIAL PET OF CLASSROOM A! CAN RUN UP WALLS! AND LICK HIS OWN EYEBALL!

ANGELINA, AKA WONDER PIG! OFFICIAL PET OF CLASSROOM B. REALLY GOOD AT MAZES! ALSO POSSESSES SUPER-HAMSTER STRENGTH!

CLEVER, AKA THE GREEN WINGER. OFFICIAL PET OF CLASSROOM D! SHE FLIES! ALSO, CAN EAT HALF HER WEIGHT IN BIRDSEED!

NELL, AKA FANTASTIC FISH! OFFICIAL PET OF, UH, THE HALLWAY. SHE CAN BREATHE UNDERWATER! AND SHE DRIVES THE FANTASTIC FISH TANK!

WARREN, AKA PROFESSOR TURTLE. OFFICIAL PET OF THE SCIENCE LAB! HE'S REALLY SMART . . . BUT REALLY SLOOOW.

FRANK, AKA BOSS BUNNY! PAMPERED PERSONAL PET OF PRINCIPAL BRICKFORD! HE CAN SMELL TROUBLE! AND HE HAS A SUPERBELT! WITH SUPERSTUFF IN IT!

And, of course, there was Super Turbo.

The Great Gecko stood before the rest of the Superpet Superhero League. "As you know, tonight is a superspecial meeting of the Superpet Superhero League. Tonight is

the night our newest member joins
the team . . ."

PENELOPE! SHE CAN CHANGE COLOR AND BLEND IN TO
HER SURROUNDINGS, BECOMING INVISIBLE!

"It's about time we made it official!" said Wonder Pig "Penelope's
been one of us for months!"

"That's true," said the Great Gecko. "And until now, Penelope has never had a superhero name. You can't be a proper member of the Superpet Superhero League without a proper superhero name!"

Penelope stood next to the Great Gecko. "It's been really hard to come up with a superhero name for myself," she said.

Super Turbo nodded in agreement. Coming up with a good superhero name was a tricky business. After all, his own superhero name was just his real name, with the word *super* in front of it.

Penelope continued. "That's why I asked each of you to come up with a suggestion. I'll choose the one that fits me best!"

The Superpets went around the room, each

offering their ideas.

"Leaping Lizard!" cried Fantastic Fish.

"What?! What's wrong?" said Boss Bunny frantically.

"No, no, that's my idea for Penelope's superhero name!" Fantastic Fish said, trying to calm Boss Bunny.

"That's great," said Penelope, "but I'm not much of a leaper."

The Green Winger thought the Invisible Sneaker was a good name.

The Great Gecko pointed out that that made Penelope sound like a shoe.

Boss Bunny came up with the Secret Ingredient.

"Oh, Frank, you're always thinking of food," the Green Winger said with a laugh.

Professor Turtle suggested calling Penelope hidden P, because you would never know she was there, like the hidden *p* in the word pterodactyl. Everyone agreed that while it was very clever, that name would have to be explained every time someone heard it for the first time, and evil simply doesn't wait for such things.

Wonder Pig suggested calling her Clear Isabelle—get it? Clear. As. A. Bell?—but Penelope thought it would be a little confusing to have two different first names.

"Uh, I thought maybe . . . Captain Chameleon?" Super Turbo offered up.

"Captain Chameleon!" repeated Penelope, testing it out. "I like it!"

"It's always helpful to know exactly what species of Superpet

you're dealing with," added Boss Bunny, approvingly.

"Captain Chameleon it is!" yelled the

Great Gecko, who was happy to change the subject.

3

IT'S OFFICIAL!

"All right, now let's begin the swearing-in ceremony!" said the Great Gecko.

The Superpets lined up on either side of Penelope and the Great Gecko.

PLEASE REPEAT AFTER ME.

The Superpets erupted in cheers. "That was the most beautiful ceremony I've ever seen," said Fantastic Fish, drying an eye.

"Well, that's it! Welcome to the Superpets, Captain Chameleon!" said the Great Gecko. "Normally I'd say this would be an occasion for a party, but tonight's a school night, and we all need to get back to our classrooms."

"Good thing tomorrow night isn't!" yelled Wonder Pig. "Party in Classroom C!"

"Exactly! And everyone has their assignments for tomorrow night's party, right?" the Great Gecko asked, looking around.

The Superpets nodded.

"Super!" said the Great Gecko. "See you all tomorrow!"

And with that, the Superpets scampered back to their cages, tanks, and terrariums.

4

SNACK RUN!

Super Turbo sat in his cage and let out a deep breath. The school day was finally over! He loved his kids but they could be a handful. Plus, the end of the day meant that it was almost party time!

The second-grade teacher, Ms. Beasley, packed up her bag as the janitor finished cleaning up a paint-glitter-feather-ice pop mess one of the kids had made.

"I'm sorry again about the mess, Mr. Wilson," said Ms. Beasley to the janitor.

"No worries, Ms. B.," said the janitor. "I've had to clean up way worse messes in the cafeteria lately. Have a good weekend," he said as he left the room.

Ms. Beasley turned off the lights. "See ya, Turbo," she called as she left. Of course, she had no idea her class's pet hamster could actually under-stand her.

When the coast was clear, Turbo sprang into action. He only had a few hours until the party began! He ran down the checklist.

THE GREEN WINGER AND THE GREAT GECKO WERE ON DECORATIONS.

CONGRATS CAP'N CHAMEL'N!

WONDER PIG AND FANTASTIC FISH WERE ON LIGHTS.

PROFESSOR TURTLE WAS GOING TO SUPPLY THE MUSIC.

BOSS BUNNY HAD VOLUNTEERED
TO HELP CLEAN UP.

AND TURBO WAS IN CHARGE OF
GETTING SNACKS.

Getting snacks for a party like this was no small matter. It was more of a supermatter!

"Psst! Hey," came a whispery voice from behind him. "Psst!"

Super Turbo wheeled around, ready for action. Instead he found . . . Boss Bunny?

"And also, you can get yourself some extra snacks before the party, right?" Super Turbo asked with a knowing smile.

"There is also that, yes," Boss Bunny replied.

Normally when the Superpets needed to move around the school they used the vent system.

But since the school was now empty, Super Turbo and Boss Bunny

simply headed down the hallway to the cafeteria.

Boss Bunny was picturing all the snacks that awaited them. "And we can get some onion crackers, and we can get some peanut butter cookies, and we can get some of those little tiny baby carrots, and we can get some—oh no!"

"Ono? What's ono?" asked Super Turbo.

"No, I meant, 'oh no, look at the cafeteria door!'" said Boss Bunny, pointing.

"Oh no" was right! The cafeteria door was locked for the weekend!

Luckily, Super Turbo was a quick thinker.

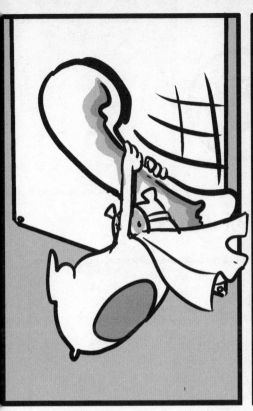

"Wow," said Boss Bunny, clapping his little bunny paws together. "That was really super, Super Turbo!"

Super Turbo smiled. "Now let's get some snacks!"

5

THE SMELL OF DANGER

Super Turbo and Boss Bunny stepped into the cafeteria.

"Smell any trouble?" asked Super Turbo. He figured he could at least *pretend* that's why Boss Bunny was there.

"Not yet!" said Boss Bunny as he bounded over to the cafeteria's pantry.

The door to the pantry was slightly ajar already.

"Well, that's lucky!" said Super Turbo as they scurried inside.

Neither of them noticed the door close quietly behind them. Boss Bunny ran to and fro, his mouth watering so much that he actually slipped on his own drool. "They must have just restocked in here! Oh boy, oh boy, oh boy!"

Super Turbo licked his lips. So many wonderful snacks! "Okay, we need a plan!" he said. "First thing we have to do is figure out how to get this stuff out of here!"

"I can carry about twelve cookies in my belly," said Boss Bunny, ripping open a package.

"Aha!" Super Turbo had an idea. He pulled out a packet of tortillas, tore it open, and threw one on the floor. "We'll pile everything we want to bring on top of that!" he said, pointing. "Then we can drag it back to Classroom C!"

"Gooff ideaff, Suffperff Turffboff!" said Boss Bunny, his mouth full.

When Boss Bunny was finished chewing, he and Super Turbo gathered all the things they wanted for Captain Chameleon's party.

THEY GOT THESE.

YuM-O's

THOSE.

SOME OF THESE.

WONDER PIG REALLY LIKES THESE.

ONE OF THOSE.

THIS IS PENELOPE'S—ER, CAPTAIN CHAMELEON'S—FAVORITE!

A WHOLE BUNCH OF THESE.

"Wow!" said Super Turbo, "That's a lot of food!"

"Yeah!" said Boss Bunny, throwing a bag of chips on top. "This party is going to be awesome!"

Suddenly, Boss Bunny stopped and sniffed the air.

"What is it, Boss Bunny? Trouble?" Super Turbo asked.

"Depends on what trouble smells like," said Boss Bunny, still sniffing. "Because this smells like dirty socks."

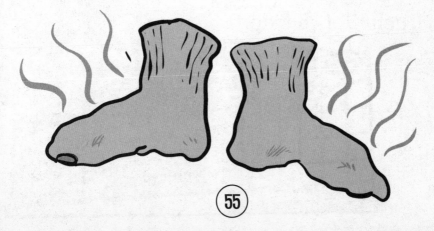

Super Turbo breathed in. Now he could smell it too. He looked around. Boss Bunny was moving closer to some sort of box that was on the ground. He was getting closer—and closer—and—

"Stop!" Super Turbo cried. "Boss Bunny, I think that's a trap," he said. And now that he was closer, he could see that the cagelike box was *definitely* a trap.

"Well that trap smells worse than the time Principal Brickford left an egg salad sandwich in the waste basket before going home for the weekend. I'm not going anywhere near that thing!"

Phew! Crisis averted.

The two Superpets ran over to their towering pile of snacks and started dragging the tortilla toward the pantry's exit.

"Oof, this is heavy!" said Super Turbo.

"Should've ... gone a bit lighter ...
on the cookies,"wheezed Boss Bunny.
Suddenly Boss Bunny stood up
straight, sniffing the air again.

"Oh no, what is
it now?" asked
Turbo. "Is it that
terrible smell? Or is it ...
danger?"

"Neither!" said Boss Bunny,
excitedly. "It smells like ...
cashew butter! My favorite!"

"It's coming from in there!"
said Boss Bunny, pointing to
a different box, but very much like

the one that the stinky smell was coming from.

"I don't think we should go in there. It looks—" Super Turbo began, but Boss Bunny was already off and running. The next thing he knew, Boss Bunny was in the box . . . and so was Super Turbo.

"Wow, Look at that!" said Boss
Bunny "A big blob of cashew butter
just sitting there!"

"Wait!" cried Super Turbo. "Don't touch it, Boss Bunny! I think it may be a—"

SNAP!

6

SUPER TURBO BEHIND BARS

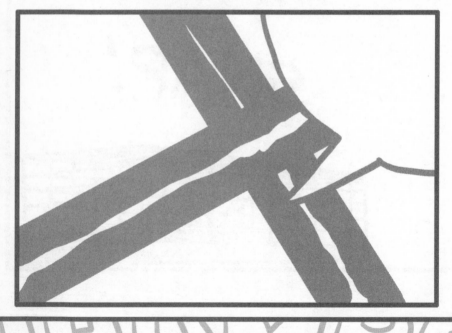

"—trap," finished Super Turbo.

Boss Bunny touching the cashew butter had triggered the door to snap shut behind them. Now they were . . . trapped.

WHAT DO WE DO?!

WELL, I'M SEEING TWO OF YOU NOW . . .

"This is terrible!" cried Boss Bunny. "I'm too adorable to be trapped! Who would want to trap us, anyway?"

"Boss Bunny, we have to try to remain calm. We have to think," said Super Turbo.

Super Turbo twirled his whiskers thoughtfully. "I wonder," he began. "Could it be? Could it be that these traps weren't meant for us? That they're here to catch Whiskerface and his Rat Pack because the rats were spotted in the cafeteria?"

"Those dirty rats!" wailed Boss Bunny, shaking the bars of the trap as hard as he could.

"Boss Bunny, it's okay!" said Super Turbo reassuringly. "Once the janitor sees us caught in the traps, he'll just put us back in our nice, comfy cages," explained Super Turbo.

"I think you're forgetting something," said Boss Bunny. "It's Friday night. The janitor won't be in until Monday morning. We're going to be stuck here all weekend! We're going to starve! Our fingers might fall off! And—" He suddenly gasped. "We're going to miss the party!"

Something dawned on Super Turbo too. "If the janitor comes in

here and sees us in our superhero costumes, he's going to know that we're secretly Boss Bunny and Super Turbo!"

"NOT OUR SECRET IDENTITIES!" screamed Boss Bunny. In a flash, he pulled off his utility belt and hurled it and all its contents through a space between the bars of the trap. "Quick, Super Turbo, take off your cape and goggles too! If we're not

wearing our costumes he won't be able to tell we're superheroes!"

7

IT GETS WORSE

"Well, well, well," said someone from the darkness. "If it isn't
Booger Bunny and Stinky Turbo!"

"Whiskerface!" Super Turbo said
through gritted teeth. It was bad
enough that he and Boss Bunny
were trapped. Now their arch-
enemy was here too!

"It's your fault we're caught!" yelled back Super Turbo. "These traps are here because you rats keep stealing food from the cafeteria!"

"My fault?!" Whiskerface leaned in to the bars of the trap. "It's you Superpests who keep stealing all the food! For your meetings and your parties!"

"We're rats! We know we're not wanted here in Sunnyview Elementary. We keep a low profile, so no one notices us. If someone put out traps, it's because you guys keep taking so many snacks!"

Super Turbo opened his mouth to say something, but nothing came out. It was true, the Superpets did take a lot of snacks from the cafeteria.

"Are you going to let us out?" asked Boss Bunny.

"NO!" erupted Whiskerface. "Because you guys weren't being careful, now the Rat Pack and I are in danger! So, no, I'm not going to let you out!"

Suddenly Whiskerface stood up straight and sniffed the air. "Wait, what is that?"

Boss Bunny and Super Turbo both
sniffed the air.

"All I smell is that awful garbage
gym socks smell," said Boss Bunny.

"It smells . . . delicious!" said
Whiskerface, almost in a daze. He

started drifting off toward where the smell was coming from.

Super Turbo realized what was happening. "No, Whiskerface! Don't! You'll get caught in the—"

8

AND EVEN WORSE

Whiskerface stuffed the last bit of stinky cheese into his mouth. "I may have been too hasty in not offering to help you guys earlier."

"Ugh, I can't believe you're eating that!" said Boss Bunny, holding his nose. "It smells like a skunk and a garbage can got into a burping contest."

"You don't know what you're talking about." Whiskerface looked at Boss Bunny. "The smell, it over-came me! I couldn't help myself!"

"Well, now we're all trapped!" Super Turbo pointed out.

"Yeah, we are," said Whiskerface, peering around his cage. "Oh boy, this is bad. . . ."

Super Turbo hadn't thought of that. The worst that would happen to him and Boss Bunny is they might be exposed as superheroes. But for Whiskerface and the rest of the Rat Pack, the stakes were much higher! Super Turbo felt awful. If Whiskerface was right, the whole reason the traps were there in the first place was because the Superpets kept raiding the cafeteria for snacks.

Super Turbo looked over at Whiskerface. Was he . . . crying?

"There . . . there . . . ," Super Turbo said awkwardly. "When the rest of the Superpets see that Boss Bunny and I aren't at the party—"

"And with no snacks—" added Boss Bunny.

"They're sure to come looking for us, and once they do, they'll free all three of us!" said Super Turbo, smiling.

"All we have to do is sit tight and wait! I'm sure they'll notice us missing. Any second now! Yep, any second now they'll walk into this pantry . . ."

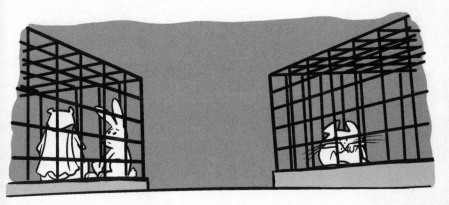

9

THE WORST YET

"How long has it been?" Boss Bunny asked Super Turbo. "I feel like we've been trapped here for hours! Maybe days! It must be Saturday by now!

Super Turbo glanced up at the clock. "It's been, uh, four minutes."

"Uh-oh," said Boss Bunny.

"What's wrong?" asked Super Turbo.

"I have to go the bathroom," replied Boss Bunny, hopping on one leg.

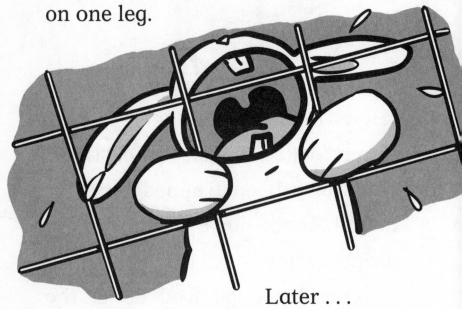

Later . . .

"That's it!" cried Boss Bunny, clutching the bars of the trap. "I can't stand it anymore! We've got to get out of here. Now!"

Super Turbo glanced up at the clock again. He and Boss Bunny hadn't even been trapped for half an hour. But in the half hour, they'd gone over every inch of the trap. And they saw no way out from inside the trap.

But outside . . .

Super Turbo looked over at Boss Bunny's utility belt. It was too far for them to reach, but it looked like

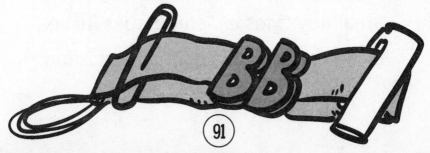

it was fairly close
to the trap that
Whiskerface
was stuck in.

"Whiskerface! Hey,
Whiskerface!" he called.

Whiskerface looked up from
the corner he'd been sitting in. "What
do you want?"

"I was thinking, we *could* sit here
for who knows how long and hope
somebody finds us," said Super Turbo,
"or we could work *together*, and find

a way out of these traps right now."

"Work together, huh?" said Whiskerface. "How so?"

"Look over there," said Super Turbo, pointing. "That's Boss Bunny's utility belt. It's full of tools to help get us out of here. It's too far for me to reach, but you might be able to grab it."

"I see," said Whiskerface, stroking his whiskers the same way Super Turbo did when he was thinking. "If I get it, how do you know I won't just

use it to free myself and leave you guys here?"

Super Turbo looked over at the rat. "I guess I don't. It's just . . . well, it's just that we all ended up here by not looking out for each other. So it makes sense that the way to get out would be by *helping* each other."

Whiskerface set his beady eyes on Super Turbo and Boss Bunny. It was so hard to read his expression! Then he reached his tiny little hand out as far as he could.

Super Turbo and Boss Bunny quickly released Whiskerface from his trap as well.

"I wasn't sure you would actually free me," admitted Whiskerface. "We aren't exactly best buds. I mean, you've ruined my plans to take over the school and then take over the

world, like, a bajillion times. And I know I've caused you a fair share of trouble."

Super Turbo reached out and put an arm around Whiskerface. "You sure have. But this time it was the Superpets who caused the trouble. It wasn't fair for you to be punished

for it. Now come on, let's bust out of here!"

"Small problem, guys. The pantry door is closed," Boss Bunny pointed out.

"Follow me," said Whiskerface. "I know a shortcut."

Super Turbo and Boss Bunny followed Whiskerface, and before they knew it, they were out of the pantry. That's right. They were out of the pantry . . . but right in the middle of a ginormous standoff between the Superpet Superhero League and the Rat Pack!

10

FRIENDS + ENEMIES = FRENEMIES?

"Whoa, whoa, whoa!" Super Turbo ran into the middle of everyone. "What's going on here?!"

"Super Turbo!" cried Captain Chameleon. "You're okay!"

"Whiskerface!" yelled one of the Rat Pack. "You're okay!"

"I'm okay too," added Boss Bunny.

"We were busy getting ready for the party and then Captain Chameleon noticed you weren't there!" said the Great Gecko to Super Turbo. "We went searching for you and then we ran into these rats stealing a whole bunch of snacks!"

"We were worried the Rat Pack had kidnapped you!" added Green Winger.

"Didn't anybody notice I was missing too?" asked Boss Bunny.

"We thought you were late so you wouldn't have to help set up," said Fantastic Fish.

"Hmm, that's fair," Boss Bunny said, nodding.

Super Turbo turned to Whisker-face. "And I would like to officially invite you and the whole Rat Pack to a party in Classroom C."

Whiskerface's beady eyes welled up. "You're inviting us . . . to *your* party?" he asked.

"Sure!" said Super Turbo. "Tonight's party was already a celebration of one new friend. Now it can be a celebration of a whole bunch of new friends!"

"For tonight at least," added the Great Gecko, sliding over to Super Turbo and Whiskerface. "Because if you and the Rat Pack ever try to take over the school again, and by extension, the world—"

"I still don't get how that will work," said Fantastic Fish.

"—then the Superpet Superhero League

will be ready to stop you!" finished the Great Gecko. "But for tonight, let's party!"